I0622482

Beautifully Valentined

Candied Crush #22

Charity Parkerson

Copyright

THE SCANNING, UPLOADING, AND distributing of this book via the internet or via any other means without the permission of the copyright owner is illegal and punishable by law. Criminal copyright infringement, including infringement without monetary gain, is investigated by the FBI and is punishable by up to 5 years in federal prison and a fine of $250,000. Please purchase only authorized electronic editions, and do not take part in or encourage electronic piracy of copyrighted materials. Brief passages may be quoted for review purposes if credit is given to the copyright holder. Your support of the author's rights is appreciated. Any resemblances to person(s) living or dead, is completely coincidental. All items contained within this novel are products of the author's imagination.

—Warning: This book is intended for readers over the age of 18. Some of my books contain allusions to past abuse and trauma. I try to have nothing triggering on page and treat every situation with care.

Copyright © 2023 Charity Parkerson

Editor: BZ Hercules & Consultants

Cover art by: Covers by Jo

CHARITY PARKERSON

All rights reserved.

Contents

Introduction

MARCO HAS SPENT HIS *entire life hungry for something he can't name. Valentine knows exactly what he needs: to be brought to his knees.*

A few years back, Marco ruined his relationship with his twin, Enzo. At one time, they stayed glued at the hip. Now Marco is determined to reclaim that connection, except he doesn't even know who he is anymore and that's getting in the way of restarting his life. There's also this cocky boxer who thinks he knows everything. He won't give Marco the space he needs to think. Now Marco doesn't know if he's in L.A. for Enzo or this ridiculous guy who won't get out of the way.

Valentine freely admits he's a bit much. He doesn't let that bother him. Having money, looks, and fame goes to a person's head. It's all part of the image. Marco is just another game. It's called getting Valentined. Plenty of men and women have been there. Marco is the first one Valentine can't shake. It's a conundrum. He's sure it'll pass.

Beautifully Valentined is the twenty-second book in Charity Parkerson's Candied Crush series where the men are like candy—rich, irresistible, and bad for your health.

Chapter One

THE PEOPLE INSIDE THE Aviator—one of the hottest clubs in L.A. — were crammed, asshole to elbow, and no one seemed to care. Marco couldn't breathe. His twin brother, Enzo, owned the exclusive nightclub. That was the only reason Marco had come tonight and currently endured the stifling body heat. Once upon a time, Marco had been set to be co-owner of this club, but Marco was the dumb twin. Always had been. Instead of moving to L.A. with his brother, and settling down with money being shoveled his way, Enzo had decided to stay in the military. That all changed eight months ago. Because life enjoyed a good laugh at Marco's expense, he had taken a hard spill down a flight of stairs on a naval carrier and broken his leg in three places. After four surgeries and too many pins, Marco was as healed as he would ever be, and his Navy career was over. Like he said, he was the dumb twin. It was too late to cry about it now.

Despite the thick crowd inside the club, Enzo had secured Marco a stool. Marco sat on the edge, holding a lukewarm beer while watching Enzo grind against his husband on the dance floor. Enzo had married Aric two years ago and hadn't looked back. Marco couldn't blame the guy. Aric was tiny and beautiful beyond words. But Marco still missed the brother Enzo had been before Aric, and he hated himself for that tiny sliver of jealousy. Before Aric, Enzo and Marco had been joined at the hip. They had done everything together, including sharing partners. Those had been some wild days. Now Marco was just Marco and Enzo was some dude's husband. Marco had moved here to be close to his twin and yet nothing felt the same. It was Marco's fault for a lot of reasons. Too many to name, really. All Marco had now was regrets. That was pretty much the theme of his existence.

"You should stop staring at them like that. Aric already thinks you hate him."

Marco's gaze moved to the man who appeared at his side and had spoken against his ear. He stared at a face he had seen hundreds of times on TV, during boxing matches and news clips. Valentine Hollinger was even bigger in person. With his dark hair shaved down the sides into a Mohawk and his brown eyes locked on Marco, he was almost terrifying. He was overwhelming. Marco could understand why no one would want to face him in the ring. Still, Marco couldn't let that comment stand.

"Aric knows I don't hate him. At least, he should." Marco had to shout the words over the music.

Valentine cupped his ear and leaned closer like he couldn't hear Marco.

Marco yelled the words again. "I said, Aric knows I don't hate him."

Valentine shook his head and snagged Marco's beer. Before Marco could balk, Valentine towed Marco to his feet. He set the beer bottle on the stool where Marco had been. "Come on. We'll dance while you explain why you hate your brother-in-law."

It was too much. First off, Marco didn't know this guy. Not really. Second, he didn't like being manhandled. "Nah. I think I'll pass, since you can't even bother introducing yourself."

Laughter danced in Valentine's eyes. "You think I haven't had that game played on me a million times? All right. I'll humor you. I'm Valentine. Would you like to dance?"

Too late, Marco realized Valentine probably did run into people every day who pretended not to know him, hoping to be different from everyone else. Still, that hadn't been his plan. He held out his hand for Valentine to shake. "Marco."

Valentine tried and failed to look serious as he shook Marco's hand. "It's nice to meet you. Enzo had told me all about you."

They had to keep taking turns leaning close to each other to shout near each other's ear to be heard. Marco hadn't failed to notice that Valentine smelled fucking amazing. Since both of Marco's brothers had a lot of money, Marco had spent a lot of time around famous people. He knew what millions smelled like. Yet Marco wasn't immune, and he hated that. He still tried to remain cordial and seemingly unaffected. "If Enzo told you all about me, then you know why I have to decline your offer to dance. My leg doesn't work like it used to, and I doubt you want to be out there with someone who moves like a robot."

As if the world conspired against him, the music slowed, and the club darkened. Even surrounded by countless people, Marco heard Valentine's wicked chuckle. "Problem solved. Let's go."

Marco did not want to do this, but Valentine had him thinking now. He didn't want Aric to think he hated him. That wasn't true at all. Aric loved Enzo and Enzo worshipped the ground Aric walked on, so Marco loved him too. He was just sad for himself and that was no one's fault but his. Marco wanted to move past the days when he couldn't get along with Aric. He needed to be a better brother.

On the dance floor, Marco experienced a flicker of discomfort. His leg protested Marco's desire to move with the music. The moment passed when Valentine engulfed him. There was no other way to describe the way Valentine took up too much space and air. Marco felt like Valentine was somehow everywhere at once. His thick arms and wide chest distracted Marco while his hands found Marco's ass. Valentine held Marco's stare so intensely, Marco couldn't decide if he wanted to look away or fall into Valentine's eyes. He was all-consuming and overwhelming. Marco's hands slid up Valentine's hard chest because he couldn't stop it from happening. He wound his arms around Valentine's neck and moved closer. Marco forgot everything. There was so much lust in Valentine's eyes. Marco needed to know if Valentine was hard for him. The power that surged through him, when their lower bodies met, nearly made Marco pant. Not only was Valentine hard, but there was also no missing how anatomically correct Valentine was. He was long and thick. Marco might have thought he was out of his league right then if he hadn't always been too cocky for his own good. The dance seemed to go on forever while they never broke eye contact. Yet Marco didn't want the moment to end.

Valentine leaned in, making Marco wonder if the guy was about to kiss him. Instead, he switched directions at the last moment and touched his mouth to Marco's ear. "Meet me in the restroom in five." He walked away with the confidence of a guy who knew Marco would obey.

Marco might have been humiliated by the abandonment except the song ended the second Valentine turned away. A surge of people left the dance floor. Marco let himself get carried along with the crowd while his brain stayed locked on the moment he had just experienced. Fuck. That dude was... wow.

Aric appeared from nowhere and linked his arms through Marco's, bringing him back to reality. "There you are. I thought I would have to arm wrestle some chick to save your stool."

A smile snapped to Marco's lips at the image Aric painted. Aric was a tiny guy with soft, short curls and delicate features. He wore tiny dresses that barely covered his junk and put everyone else to shame with his beauty. Marco couldn't imagine him in a fight.

"Thanks. You could've let her have it. I think I'll have one more quick drink and go. Agreeing to that one dance kicked my ass."

"You danced? Nice. With whom?"

Marco shrugged, strangely unwilling to admit anything. "Some dude."

Aric squeezed his arm. "Well, I appreciate you showing up tonight. Enzo has really missed you."

A genuine smile touched Marco's lips. He couldn't say Aric wasn't trying. Marco didn't deserve it. He had given Aric a hundred reasons to hate him. Marco didn't want that anymore, though. He needed a relationship with his twin. That included Aric. "Thanks for inviting me out. I'll admit I've been sitting home too much." As he said the words, a fresh wave of depression washed over him. He didn't want to go home to his empty apartment and even emptier life. Marco didn't want to flip through the channels while missing his past. He needed something he couldn't name, but he knew it didn't wait for him at home. His gaze slid toward the restroom. He missed the wild life he had lived as a pilot for the Navy. Marco craved the adrenaline of flying fighter jets at three thousand miles an hour. Butterflies stirred in his gut when he thought about the intense way Valentine had stared at him. Maybe he wasn't quite dead yet. There was at least one thing he hadn't done. One person. Marco had options other than going home to his empty apartment. It was now or never. The only problem was, he didn't know which to choose.

If Valentine knew nothing else, he knew no one would tell him no. Not for long anyhow. The only times in his life anyone had turned down a night with him, it was because they wanted to lure him into a relationship. That shit wasn't happening. But damned if ten minutes hadn't passed and Marco hadn't joined him. That had his irritation sky high. Obviously, he would find someone else to join him in no time, but that didn't mean he wasn't disappointed. Valentine had always thought Enzo was hot as fuck, but he was strictly off limits. Valentine didn't fuck with married men. Now Valentine knew there were two of him and the other one was single. Not to mention, this one had even more gorgeous eyes and a darker air about him. Valentine had to have a taste. He liked bitter snacks.

At minute fifteen, Valentine gave up. He had never waited this long for anyone. That detail alone proved how much he had wanted this one. As he opened the bathroom door, he came face to face with Marco.

Marco's palm flattened against Valentine's chest. "Did you change your mind?"

Fuck. He was sexy. "You're late."

Marco kept moving. Valentine walked backward, mesmerized by Marco's eyes. "Aric stopped me. Like you said, I don't want him to think I hate him. So I stayed to chat."

"Fair." Valentine glanced behind him. There was one stall open. He quickly hauled Marco inside before Marco got away. The moment he had the door locked, he shoved Marco against it and captured his mouth. Marco didn't play coy. He didn't pretend he didn't want Valentine as badly as Valentine wanted him. Marco came back at Valentine every bit as violently. Valentine reached down and popped open the button on his jeans and unzipped them. They were in a public restroom and didn't have all night. He wouldn't play like either of them was there for any other reason than release. Marco bit his lip.

Valentine's dick twitched. Marco was the kind of guy who would let Valentine fuck him hard. He wished he had taken the guy home instead of opting for this quick encounter. Valentine dropped his pants and sat on the toilet. He stroked his cock while he stared at Marco. "Time to show me yours."

Marco's chest heaved as if he had run for miles. He looked every bit as turned on as Valentine as he reached down and unzipped his pants. Valentine pumped his erection. It was possible he was the tiniest bit addicted to sex because Valentine full-on panted when Marco pulled out his dick.

"That's what I want." Valentine snagged Marco's waist and hauled him forward. He didn't toy with the guy. Valentine took Marco's cock to the back of his throat and didn't stop. Marco whimpered. The sound drove Valentine wild. Valentine bobbed on Marco's erection while jacking off with zero care for where they were or who heard. Marco wasn't the first guy Valentine had blown in this bathroom. He wouldn't be the last. There was no greater power than having someone's dick in his mouth. He knew, at that moment, there was nothing Marco wouldn't do as long as Valentine didn't stop.

Marco's fingers found Valentine's hair. He demanded things his way. Marco abused the back of Valentine's throat. Valentine took it. His balls drew up tight even as his throat burned from Marco's thrust. Valentine sucked hard enough to make Marco gasp. He felt Marco's muscles tense. Valentine held his breath and pumped his cock as fast as he could. He had to get to the edge. His orgasm hit and Valentine tried his best to catch the cum with his shirt even as hot cum filled his mouth. For a moment, the world went quiet. Valentine wasn't in the spotlight. He was as human as he could get. The peace would end soon. It always did. There was never any real relief. But

BEAUTIFULLY VALENTINED

Marco had given him this moment, and Valentine would take it.

Chapter Two

THE BACK PORCH WAS an every-one-knows-your-name coffee shop that had become Marco's favorite place since moving to California. For the most part, he was left in peace to enjoy his coffee while he watched the people around him. There was a gorgeous throuple who had breakfast there each day. Two of the men were dark-haired and matched each other in every way, while their third was an ethereal blond who offset them to perfection. Marco didn't know why his gaze always found them and lingered, but he couldn't help himself. He wondered how they ended up together and how they made things work. The three of them looked so in love. It was beautiful. Then there was the owner of The Back Porch. His husband often joined him at the coffee shop. Marco never really spoke to anyone, but he recognized both men from their faces alone. The owner, Wrecker, had once been a well-known football player. His husband, Johnny, was a famous singer. It was odd to see the pair living such a normal life where no one bothered them. Then again, that was L.A. in a nutshell.

Marco lifted his cup to his lips and continued people watching while doing his best to forget last night. He still couldn't believe Valentine fucking Hollinger had blown him in the bathroom of his brother's club. It was almost surreal.

Marco had done a lot of crazy things and had countless one-night stands, but none of those had been with someone famous. The experience burrowed under his skin more than he liked. As dumb as he knew he was being, there had been a moment—right before he had filled Valentine's mouth with cum—that Marco had dreamed. A completely ridiculous desire to be seen with Valentine had washed over him. He imagined a life of jealous glances tossed his way as everyone realized he had captured one of the hottest men on the planet. Then the night had ended, and they had gone their separate ways without as much as a goodbye. For the first time in Marco's life, he felt used. For nowhere near the first time, especially lately, Marco felt unimportant. Disposable. He needed to stare at the couples in the room and remind himself that love existed in all its beautiful forms.

Maybe not for him, but happiness existed elsewhere. Life wasn't pointless for everyone.

"You beat me here."

Marco smiled as Enzo filled the booth across from him. "Yeah. I had a job interview this morning. When it ended, I decided to go ahead and head this way. My veins needed the extra coffee."

Enzo glanced behind him and motioned at Wrecker. Wrecker nodded and got started on Enzo's regular order. Enzo focused on Marco again. "What's the job?"

"An office position at an insurance company for military families. It's not much, but it sounded easy."

"How did the interview go?"

At Enzo's question, Marco shrugged. There had been a lot of people waiting to be interviewed. He knew from experience that meant he wouldn't get hired. Marco didn't have the heart to admit that to Enzo. "Fine, I guess."

Enzo blew out a sigh. "I wish you'd let me help."

Marco took a sip of his coffee to wash down his bitterness before responding. "I'm good. I still have a hefty savings built up plus all my pension. If I don't get this one, I'll keep looking."

"The offer still stands for a position at the club."

Marco fought an eye twitch. "No. Thank you, though. I can't stand up all night and I'm not looking for a pity job." Not to mention, it was his own goddamn fault he wasn't a partner in the club to begin with. They had agreed to move to L.A. together and open a bar. When the time had come, Marco had been incapable of giving up the military. Flying fighter jets had been his calling in life. Now it was gone. He had first lost his best friend by refusing to leave the military, and then life had taken the legs out from beneath him—literally. His current situation was completely on him. Pride was a funny thing. He couldn't accept Enzo's help. Not to mention, he wouldn't risk Enzo thinking Marco was only here to get a piece of the pie. He wanted his twin and best friend back. Marco wanted to put in the work to get it.

"There are plenty of things you could do that wouldn't have you standing up all night."

Marco smiled, ready to decline again, when a familiar figure caught his eye. Valentine shoved his way into Enzo's side of the booth.

"Good morning, gorgeous. Where's that adorable husband of yours? I love seeing him blush when I try to convince him to sit on my knee."

The genuine smile that lit Enzo's face said it all. He liked Valentine and was happy to see him. "Hey. He's at work."

"Oh, yeah. I forgot he works for that British guy. The hot one. I can't recall his name."

"Baker."

"Yeah. That one." Valentine met Marco's stare. "Good morning."

Marco fought a smile. It humored him for someone like Valentine to be awkward for any reason. "Good morning."

"How are you?"

He was so formal with Marco. Marco treated him the same. "Good, and you?"

Valentine nodded. "Good. I'm good." Valentine glanced behind him and brightened. "Aw, shit. Let me go bug my friend, Wrecker, real quick."

Marco watched Valentine jump from the booth, cross the room, and head behind the counter like he owned the place. His gaze followed Valentine's every move as he tackled Wrecker. The two hugged and smiled like old friends. Marco couldn't look away. He recalled the way Valentine had stared up at him as he sucked Marco's dick. Marco couldn't shake Valentine's expression while he came. He had looked... real. Marco didn't know how else to explain what he had seen, but he couldn't un-see it.

"On my god. You got Valentined."

Marco's gaze shot Enzo's way. "What?"

Enzo looked stunned. He blinked like an owl. "You got Valentined," he repeated, as if saying it twice would make the words make sense.

"I don't know what in the hell you're talking about."

Enzo motioned Valentine's way without ever looking away from Marco. "You hooked up with Valentine in the bathroom of my club, didn't you?"

Marco's eyebrows rose. That was some specific bullshit... as if it was something that happened three times a night at The Aviator.

Enzo didn't even wait for Marco to confirm his suspicions. "Oh my god. You did."

Marco panicked. He had known the encounter hadn't meant anything, but he hadn't suspected he was just one of many on a nightly basis. Marco hadn't known there was a goddamn name for it. His mind raced. He had to get away before Valentine returned. Marco startled and dug out his phone as if he had gotten an unexpected notification. He checked the face, pretending to read.

"Damn. I have to go. That place I interviewed for this morning wants me to come back in for some follow-up questions."

Enzo eyed him, as if he knew he had lied. "Okay. Good luck. Let me know how it goes."

"I will." Marco pulled out his wallet.

Enzo waved it away. "I've got it. You go ahead. You don't want to lose out on the job because you got held up here."

Marco flashed Enzo a grateful smile. "Thank you. I'll catch you next time."

Marco didn't stick around to see if Enzo agreed. He had to get out of there before Valentine returned. There were enough things in his life humbling him at the moment. Marco didn't need Valentine laughing at him too. He should have known someone like Valentine wouldn't want him for real. Marco had simply been a new face in a club where he had likely already made the rounds twice. He couldn't be dumber. So much for reclaiming his life. He may as well have stuck his dick in a glory hole. At least then he would have known he wasn't really wanted. Marco wouldn't make the same mistake twice. He would stay far away from Valentine from now on. He wouldn't be made a fool of twice. Marco could do that all by himself.

Valentine turned his head in just enough time to watch Marco limp out the door. His sexy shoulders filled out his dress shirt and his pants shaped the perfect ass. It was almost painful to watch him walk. Marco couldn't completely bend one leg and it broke Valentine's heart to watch him. He was an eagle with clipped wings. That was something Valentine understood way better than the world knew. Maybe that was why he fought the urge to run after him. He didn't have any reason to apologize, but he still felt like he should.

When Valentine had walked through the door, he had spotted Enzo right away and Marco second. That was only because Marco had his back to the door. He didn't know why he had been incapable of walking past without speaking. It wasn't like they were friends or anything. That goddamn limp, though. Then there was the pure bitterness in Marco's eyes. That was another thing they had in common. The difference was no one knew about Valentine's pain. For all the people he called friend, there wasn't a soul that truly fit the title. People didn't have friends when they got to the top. All they had were climbers, looking for a leg up or hand out. So Valentine took what he wanted and fuck everyone else. There was no reason for him to care when no one concerned themselves with him. Not really.

Still, he couldn't stop dreaming of a real connection. After some small talk with Wrecker, Valentine made his way back to Enzo. Enzo looked lost in thought as Valentine slid into the booth across from him.

"We lost one."

Enzo blinked, as if coming out of a daze. "Yeah. Marco had a job interview."

Valentine nodded and rearranged the sugar packets in their container so all the colors were in order. "He doesn't have a job?"

"Not since leaving the Navy, no. His leg is too damaged to do most jobs, because nearly everything requires at least a little manual labor. He also doesn't qualify for disability because of his pension." Enzo pulled an annoyed face. "And he's too fucking stubborn to accept a job from me. That's making it hard for him to find anything."

That sucked. "Well, maybe he'll have some luck today."

Enzo stared at him for a moment in silence, making Valentine uncomfortable. He almost cracked a joke to break the tension. Enzo didn't give him time. "Don't play with my brother, okay?"

A laugh burst from Valentine in his discomfort. "Which one? Don't you have one of those huge Italian families?"

Enzo didn't smile. "I'm being serious. I like you, but Marco has been through a lot this past year. He doesn't need someone toying with his feelings on top of everything else."

Valentine had a hard time being serious. He didn't like anyone seeing beneath his armor. "Your twin doesn't seem like the type who needs protecting. I'm pretty sure he can hold his own. Isn't he the player of you two?"

Enzo's chest expanded on a deep breath, as if calling on some inner fortitude to tolerate Valentine. "Whatever. Never mind. I guess I've forgotten what it was like to be single and give no fucks about anyone other than myself. I'm sure you two have this."

Ouch. He deserved that, but still. "I'm glad you feel that way. You should give me his number." Because Valentine didn't like being told what to do.

Anger flashed in Enzo's eyes. "You know what? What the fuck ever. Get out your phone."

Valentine dutifully pulled out his phone.

"Five. Five. Five. Eight. Two. Nine. Three. I suppose you want me to pay for your goddamn coffee too."

A smile snapped to Valentine's lips. He was oddly happy to have gotten Marco's number. "Nah. I'll buy."

"Good. You're picking up Marco's order too, then."

Whatever. He was good. Valentine had Marco's number, and all was right in his world. Money meant nothing in this transaction. Valentine just wanted to see Marco again. They had at least one more night in them. Valentine felt that in his soul.

Chapter Three

LIKELY SPAM: *HEY, IT'S Valentine. I have a quick question for you.*

Marco: *Why is your number showing up as "likely spam" and how did you get my number?*

Valentine: *I don't know. Save it and fix the problem. Enzo gave me your number. Anyhow, what are you doing right now?*

Marco: *Watching TV.*

Valentine: *Can you fly a Dassault Falcon 900?*

Marco: *I can fly anything.*

Valentine: *I mean legally? Like do you have a valid pilot's license?*

Marco: *Yes.*

Valentine: *Cool. If I pay you five grand, will you fly me to Vegas tonight, stay the night, and fly me back in the morning? I'll cover your room, meals, and all that too, of course.*

Marco: *Why me?*

Valentine: *Your brother says you're the best. I have a thing tonight in Vegas, and my pilot is sick. So what do you say?*

Marco: *Sure. Just tell me when and where. I'll be there.*

Valentine: *Sweet.*

The air that filled Marco's lungs felt like his first real breath in ages as Marco climbed to over thirty thousand feet. Marco only felt like himself when he was soaring above the clouds. Valentine's private plane was nice as hell. It was like flying a really fast limo. He glanced over to find Valentine staring at him.

"What?"

"You look happy." Valentine sounded more thoughtful than observant, making Marco uncomfortable. He wasn't used to people staring at him while he flew.

"Tell me again why you're up here with me. You have this whole plane with a bedroom and everything. There's no need to sit here."

Valentine didn't look inclined to budge. "I've never sat in the cockpit during a flight. Since it's just you and me, tonight seemed like a good time to try it out."

He supposed that was fair. It was Valentine's plane, after all. "What are your plans in Vegas?" Marco half expected Valentine to tell him it was none of his business. He just needed to talk about something else. Marco was more than a little stunned when Valentine answered without qualm.

"My manager lives in Vegas. He's been trying to drag me into another title match for months now. I keep saying no and he keeps pushing. He's asked to meet in person to discuss the details."

It went against Marco's character to be nosy, but he was too curious to keep his questions to himself. "Wouldn't it help his case if he came to you rather than making you fly to him?"

Valentine eyed Marco, looking entirely too serious. "Nothing will help his case, but he's footing the bill for this trip. I plan to squeeze every penny I can from him by making him wine and dine me before saying no."

"Why don't you want to fight?" The question was out there before Marco could stop it from happening.

Valentine shrugged. He didn't look inclined to keep talking. Marco was surprised when he did. "A lot of reasons. You want to help me spend Bryce's money? He made most of it from me anyhow."

Marco flashed Valentine a smile. Despite learning he was only one in a long line of Valentine's conquests, Marco liked him. He felt comfortable in Valentine's company. Plus, Valentine had given him back the sky. At least for tonight and once in the morning anyhow. That was priceless. "How can I help?"

Valentine's smile made the offer worthwhile. "Stick by my side tonight. Whatever I get, you get too. We'll make him pay double for keeping up this relentless campaign."

Marco nodded. He wasn't above spending someone else's money, especially when they were bothering his friend. That thought brought all others to a screeching halt. He didn't know Valentine. They had just met last night. Why did the guy feel like a friend? Marco had already let Valentine play him once. Then again, Marco had been using him too. Marco decided to wipe the slate clean. He enjoyed Valentine's company. Valentine was outrageous, but he was also like lightning in a jar. He lit whole rooms and brought the space to life. There was no reason to hold grudges. Marco didn't really have any friends in L.A. It was nice to dream.

"Let's see how much trouble we can start."

Valentine laughed. It was a sexy sound. He slapped Marco's shoulder. "That's my boy."

It was ridiculous how good those words felt in Marco's chest. Like last night, being in Valentine's company made Marco feel important—like he was special. Valentine was dangerous like that. Marco didn't want the feeling to stop.

Bryce Townshend had been Valentine's manager since the beginning of his career. While Bryce was good at getting Valentine all the money he was worth, they had always had a lopsided relationship. If Bryce hadn't made all the right moves with Valentine, Bryce wouldn't have gone anywhere. Valentine was the one who fought his way to the top. Bryce hadn't won all his matches. Valentine had done that. He had taken Bryce with him. Without Valentine, Bryce wouldn't have shit. Every client he had now was built on the back of Valentine's career. Valentine wished the guy would focus on his other clients, because Valentine was retiring. The world didn't know it yet, but Valentine was done. He wasn't ready. Valentine had thought he had a good ten years left in him, but no. A migraine that had caused him to lose sight in one eye and sent him to a specialist had stolen everything from him. He hadn't dealt with it. Valentine was nowhere near ready to disclose it, but

Valentine had brain damage. He would never fight again.

Bryce was on to him pretty early in the night. His light gray eyes kept flashing with rage each time Valentine left the check for him. He knew. Valentine wouldn't fold. He waited for Bryce to break down. Bryce finally found the edge of his patience while inside the hotel's casino.

"Just tell me why?"

Valentine tossed back the last of his whiskey. It burned all the way down. "What do you mean?"

Bryce looked Marco's way, as if wishing they were alone. Marco didn't take the hint and leave. He made Valentine proud. Bryce met Valentine's stare again. "We're talking about millions here, Val. Not just in bonuses and prize money, but new sponsorships. Commercials. Your face everywhere."

"My face is already everywhere."

Bryce's voice turned pleading. "This is your career. It's mine. This guy is out here calling you a coward for not facing him, and you're acting like it's nothing."

It wasn't nothing. His name meant everything to him. Cody Stewart was a fair fighter. He probably had a shot at taking Valentine. It would be a fun match, especially for the fans. He loathed the idea of letting the guy smear his name, but life didn't give a fuck about his pride. If he fought again, it might kill him, and the league would never let it happen anyhow. "Sometimes you have to go out on top."

Bryce sat forward, looking apoplectic. "What are talking about here, Val? Are you talking about retirement?"

Valentine's gaze moved to Marco.

Marco stared back. He didn't look as if he cared one way or the other about the conversation taking place around him. Valentine knew, though—if anyone would understand his plight, it was Marco. Maybe that was the real reason he had asked Marco to join him tonight. Bryce would feel zero pinch from picking up Marco's check on top of his, but Marco deserved this night out and Valentine needed one goddamn person in his corner. One fucking person who understood what it was like to lose their dream.

"I don't want to end up with dementia." Valentine held Marco's stare as he made the confession. He couldn't say it to Bryce.

Bryce scoffed. "You're nowhere near there."

Valentine's gaze moved Bryce's way. He held his stare.

Bryce's smile fell. "You're nowhere near there, right?"

Valentine didn't respond.

Bryce ran an angry hand through his dark hair, leaving it standing on end. He unexpectedly shot to his feet, knocking over his chair. Heads turned their way as Bryce stormed off. Valentine bit his tongue and stared at nothing. Emptiness filled him, sending a chill through his body. A bitter smile pulled at his lips. His gaze shifted Marco's way. Marco still held his stare with zero emotion.

Valentine took a breath. "And that's what it's like to be surrounded by people who would rather you die than cut off their money train."

Marco's mouth lifted in one corner. "At least your brother isn't trying to give you a pity position at his bar because you're too pathetic to do anything else."

A genuine smile snapped to Valentine's lips. "If I had a brother, he'd probably only want my money too. Do you want to help me clean out the mini bar in the room and run up Bryce's bill?"

Marco glanced around. There were dark circles under his eyes Valentine hadn't noticed earlier. Despite that, the guy really was gorgeous. Valentine imagined men and women tripped over themselves to talk to him. Green eyes focused on him again, catching him staring. "I saw an ice cream shop when we left the restaurant earlier. Can I buy you a milkshake instead?"

Valentine shook his head. The ugly moment with Bryce slowly faded. "Do you want me to get fat now that I can't fight anymore?"

"Do you think liquor is better?"

Valentine came to his feet. "Fair. Lead the way." He waited patiently while Marco stood. Valentine didn't miss the way Marco winced and tried to hide it. If Valentine understood anything, it was living in pain while trying to cling to his pride. He pretended not to notice anything was amiss.

As they headed outside the casino and into the hotel lobby, several people pulled out their phones and snapped pictures. If Marco noticed, he didn't show it. Valentine set his hand on the small of Marco's back and marked his territory. The move happened without thought. Valentine never aligned his name with anyone's. He was notoriously single. By tomorrow, Marco's face would be everywhere. Everyone would want to know who Valentine had been with in Vegas. It was too late to take back the move. Oddly, Valentine wouldn't if he could.

In fact, Valentine leaned closer and pressed his lips against Marco's ear. "I forgot to tell you earlier. You look hot as fuck tonight. Lickable, in fact."

Marco turned a laughing gaze Valentine's way. "Ah. There's the real you. You had me worried."

A snort escaped Valentine. Everyone else disappeared. "So, what about me?"

"What about you?" Marco never stopped smiling.

Valentine didn't either. "I said you look hot. Now it's your turn to say I look sexy. That's how it works. Tit for tat."

Somehow, Marco's smile grew. "I don't think you need anyone complimenting you. Your head might not fit through the door, and I want ice cream."

Valentine draped his arm across Marco's shoulders. "We can't have you missing that. Not to mention, if I can't fit my head through the door, then you can't take me to bed tonight, and I've been a really bad boy. I need you to spank me."

Marco released a put-upon sigh that righted everything wrong in Valentine's world. He didn't know what the future held for him. Valentine had lost the only thing he loved: his career. But he had a plan for tonight and he wasn't alone. He could live with that. It was a place to start.

Valentine's career was over. God, that punched Marco in his chest. That wasn't news that had hit the headlines yet. When it did... fuck. Marco understood, and he had seen something in Valentine as he had dropped that news on his manager. Marco's throat swelled just thinking about it. Valentine had looked the way Marco felt every time he remembered he would never fly another mission or sleep on another naval ship. Their dreams were vastly different, but equally dead, nonetheless. Obviously, Valentine would still be fine financially, but still. There was no substitute for losing the only reason for living. Marco would know.

They walked around the city, drinking their shakes and seeing the sights. Valentine had admitted, while he had been to

Vegas several times, he never came as just a tourist. Marco enjoyed being with him for his all his firsts. They saw the High Roller and went up into the Eiffel Tower viewing deck. Marco made sure Valentine saw all the highlights they feasibly could in one night. He paid for their ice cream and entry fees. The date had been Marco's idea. He would be damned if Valentine paid. They stayed out until two in the morning before heading back toward the hotel. Marco hadn't forgotten Valentine's crack about taking him to bed. In fact, it was damn near all he thought about. Truthfully, that was one of the reasons he hadn't hurried back to the hotel. He wasn't sure how he felt about going to bed with Valentine.

"I feel like I know you since I've known Enzo for so long, but then again, I barely know you at all. It's kind of weird."

Marco nodded at Valentine's observation. "I get that. Sometimes, it's strange having another person out there who looks and sounds just like me, especially since he's become a stranger the last couple of years. It's my fault," Marco rushed to add before Valentine jumped to any conclusions. Then Marco recalled Valentine's warning at The Aviator about Aric thinking Marco hated him. "I guess you know that, though."

Valentine shrugged. "Aric is chatty when he's drunk and anxious. I'm guessing you moving here made him nervous. He spilled everything to me one night while I waited with him outside the club. We were waiting on Enzo to grab some stuff from the office."

Marco fought a wince. At one time, Marco had done his best to ruin Enzo's and Aric's relationship. It had partially been a misunderstanding, but mostly, he had just been an ass. "I'm sure I came off sounding delightful in that story."

"Actually, Aric carries a lot of guilt because he knows how close Enzo used to be with you. He worries Enzo will resent him one day, if you two don't find a new way to be as close as you once were."

"Neither of us are the same people we used to be." That was all Marco could think to say. He was beyond moved that Aric hadn't made him into a bad guy. Marco didn't deserve it. Aric was a way better person than Marco would ever be. He needed to change the subject. "What about you? I feel like I know you by seeing your face everywhere, but I don't really know you."

"What do you want to know?"

He considered all the questions he could ask before deciding on one. "Do you look like your mom or your dad?"

A loud laugh burst from Valentine, making Marco smile. "I have no idea. Not only do I have two moms, neither of them are my biological parents, I'm adopted."

"Huh. I've never heard that. Not that I've looked into your past or anything," Marco rushed to add before Valentine's head got any bigger.

Valentine eyed him. "Is your leg hurting? You're limping more than usual. I didn't even think about that when you suggested this walk."

He was hurting, but—funnily enough—Marco hadn't even thought about it. Marco had been too focused on Valentine. He shrugged. "I'm always hurting. It doesn't matter."

"It does." Valentine sounded so solemn, it hit Marco in the chest. People cared about his plight, to an extent, but they didn't understand. Valentine understood. "I know." A childish light entered Valentine's eyes. Marco nearly groaned. He already knew Valentine well enough to know nothing good came of his current expression.

"I can literally see the hotel from here. There's no need for whatever it is you're thinking."

Valentine shook his head. "No. I insist. It's my fault you're in pain. I was the one who hadn't seen the sights, and so it's my responsibility to do what I can to help."

"Oh, God." The words were out before he even knew what Valentine would do. Then it was every bit as bad as he expected. In a move too quick to follow, Valentine snagged Marco's waist and easily tossed him over his shoulder. He sprinted toward the hotel, laughing like the idiot he was, while Marco had the wind knocked out of him on every bounce. Marco was a tall guy. He also wasn't a small one. Nothing about his current situation was cute or sane. Yet, despite every humiliating thing about the experience, Marco was having the best time he'd had in years. He fought a laugh. Marco couldn't even imagine how they looked to everyone else. He hid his face, silently dying while Valentine rode the elevator up to the penthouse where they were staying. As soon as they stepped off the elevator and into the room, Valentine slapped his ass hard before setting him on his feet.

Marco knew his face burned bright red in a combination of humiliation and blood rushing to his head. "What the fuck was that?" Even Marco heard the laughter in his voice.

Valentine didn't answer him. He swooped in and claimed Marco's mouth. There was no slow build. His tongue was in Marco's mouth. Marco's skin was on fire. Valentine tore at his clothes. Marco let it happen. His fingers found the hem of Valentine's shirt. He tugged, needing Valentine's skin against his. Marco felt alive in Valentine's company. It didn't matter if Valentine used him. Maybe Marco used him too. He felt better tonight than he had in years. Tomorrow wasn't promised anyhow. Marco hadn't been this happy in such a long time. He didn't want to lose the moment.

Valentine kissed a path to Marco's ear and nipped. His heavy breathing proved how badly he wanted Marco. "I want to be inside you. Will you let me?"

Marco's brain went fuzzy. "Um." He swallowed. The sensation of Valentine sucking his neck made it hard to think. "I haven't exactly had time to prep for that or anything."

Both of Valentine's hands shoved their way down the back of Marco's loosened jeans. He squeezed Marco's ass. "I don't give a fuck about none of that shit."

Marco couldn't say he gave a fuck about anything either when Valentine touched him. All he knew was he didn't want it to stop. His feet left the floor, and he found himself over Valentine's shoulder again. This time, that huge shoulder was bare, and Marco couldn't stop his hands from roaming every mile of muscle he could reach. Valentine was just solid as fuck and huge and sexy. Marco couldn't get enough. Then his back hit the bed and Valentine was everywhere. The rest of their clothes disappeared. Valentine's mouth touched every inch of Marco at some point. Marco fought for air. His mind was a mess. It was like his brain cells fired too fast to form any real thoughts. He knew Valentine wore a condom, and he knew lubed fingers stretched him, but he couldn't focus enough to recall how it happened. Then Valentine's wide crown pushed its way inside. There was pain, but he was too aroused to care. He had never felt this good.

Valentine thrust.

A cry tore from Marco.

Valentine froze. Their gazes met and held. Valentine stared into Marco's eyes as he slowly rocked inside Marco. Marco was held captive by Valentine's intensity. Just like when they had slow danced, Valentine led while Marco's body obeyed, but they never looked away from each other. Something small and uneasy lit inside Marco. A kernel of knowledge took root. Valentine possessed everything needed to destroy Marco. He felt very real to Marco. This wasn't some random guy who appeared on the cover of fitness magazines. He was a person, and he made Marco feel something. Valentine was dangerous.

The pressure built slowly, with Valentine moving at just the right angle. It should have felt weird having Valentine openly study his every reaction, as if ensuring Marco experienced the maximum amount of pleasure. There was nothing awkward when he was with Valentine. They clicked. It was like they had known each other their entire lives.

Marco fought his way closer to the edge. His entire body itched with the need to come. He wanted to look into Valentine's eyes while he blew cum all over Valentine's stomach.

"That's it, beautiful. You're almost there. Try to break me with that tight asshole. I can feel you struggling. You're so fucking hot."

Marco scratched at the blanket beneath him, trying to find purchase. Valentine pounded inside him. The sound of skin slapping skin mixed with the whine coming from the back of Marco's throat that he couldn't stop.

Valentine made a subtle change in thrusts. His muscles flexed in the sexiest show Marco had ever seen. The dam inside him broke. A cry burst from him. His fingers dug into Valentine's forearms as he tried pulling Valentine deeper. Valentine's every thrust was almost violent. Marco couldn't stop crying out his name as the ecstasy shook him to his core.

"Fuck. Yes. Goddamn, Marco." Valentine visibly strained toward release.

Marco couldn't look away.

A guttural-sounding cry reverberated from the walls as Valentine fell forward and claimed Marco's mouth. Pride filled Valentine along with something else. It felt a lot like hope. Marco had never been so scared and happy in his entire life. He would never be the same.

Chapter Four

ENZO: *WHY IN THE hell are you all over the news with Valentine?*

Marco: *He asked me to fly him to Vegas. I did, and then we hung out. End of story.*

ENZO: *I've seen the pictures. It doesn't look like the end of the story. That doesn't look like just hanging out.*

Marco: *Don't worry so much.*

Tito: *Holy shit. Did I just see a picture of Valentine fucking Hollinger running down the strip in Vegas with you over his shoulder?*

Marco: *Likely, yes.*

Tito: *Cool. He looks fun.*

Mom: *Who is Valentine? Is he Italian? That name sounds Italian. We need more strong Italian men in our family.*

Marco: *Jesus, Ma.*

Dad: *Why didn't you answer your mother? Who is Valentine?*

Marco: *He's a famous boxer.*

Dad: *Holy shit. You don't mean Valentine Hollinger? I love that guy. You have to get me his autograph.*

Marco: *For fuck's sake, Dad.*

Dad: *Is that a yes?*

Marco: *I'll see what I can do.*

Dad: *Hell yeah.*

Their names were linked in every paper. Marco couldn't leave his apartment without someone taking his picture. Everyone wanted to ask him about Valentine. Marco heard from everyone he had ever met in his life. Everyone except Valentine. He told himself it didn't matter. Marco had gone into their night together with open eyes. He had known about Valentine's games. Marco hadn't been ignorant in any way, nor could he claim he had been used. All the foreknowledge in the world didn't stop the constant aches in his chest. Each time someone said Valentine's name, his throat swelled. Valentine was out there in the world, likely fucking someone different every night. Marco was the one with the problem. He hadn't been misled. His stupid emotions had a mind of their own. Marco couldn't control a goddamn thing. That was his life in a nutshell. He was powerless.

His doorbell rang.

Marco's eyes fell closed. He took a steadying breath. He was exhausted from turning reporters away. It had been three days, and he never had a moment's peace. He had no intention of answering, but it dinged over and over again, getting faster by the second, until

Marco jumped to his feet, ready to tear off someone's head. Marco ripped open the door. A huge bundle of red roses blocked his sight.

"What the fuck?"

The roses lowered and Valentine's smiling face appeared. A smile automatically snapped to Marco's lips. Valentine brought the sunshine with him everywhere he went. "Hi."

Marco tried squelching his huge grin without luck. "Hey."

"Do I get to come in or are you still not talking to me?"

Marco automatically took a step back. "Why do you think I'm not talking to you?"

As he stepped through the door, Valentine shrugged. "I haven't heard from you, and I know reporters have been hounding you." He handed Marco the roses as Marco shut the door. "These are for you. I figured you didn't want anything else to do with me once you realized what being around me would be like for you."

Marco felt a bit dumb once he realized the truth. There was no reason he couldn't have texted or called first. It wasn't only on Valentine to reach out. He smelled the roses. No one had ever brought him flowers before. "Thank you. These are nice." They were. He didn't really know what to say or how to act, so he headed back toward the couch and set the vase on the coffee table.

Valentine followed. "I'm sorry."

Marco turned. His face screwed up in his confusion. "For what?"

Valentine shrugged, looking uncomfortable. He was adorable. His pink t-shirt protested against his every muscle, deforming the cartoon cat printed on the front. His jeans were loose in the waist because they were way too tight on his thick thighs. Marco took in every detail. The truth hit him. No matter how many minutes of his time Valentine gave Marco, it would never be enough.

"I'm not upset in any way. Reporters have been hounding me, but it's not like I have anywhere to be, so..." Marco shrugged. "I should've called so you didn't worry."

Valentine smiled. He reminded Marco of a giant kid. "So I was thinking."

Marco groaned.

Valentine's smile somehow got bigger. "What?"

"When you've been thinking, it ends up with you running down the street with me tossed over your shoulder. Your thoughts scare me." Marco sat on the couch and stared up at Valentine, waiting to be told he was wrong to worry.

Instead, Valentine twisted his fingers, looking nervous. Marco's curiosity shot through the roof. Valentine didn't continue.

Marco gestured for him to spill. "You were thinking..."

"Everyone thinks we're a couple."

Marco's eyebrows rose.

Valentine bit his bottom lip.

Again, Marco motioned for him to spit it out.

Valentine blew out a sigh. "I mean everyone already believes we're a couple. So we should be, don't you think?"

Marco's mind blanked.

Valentine kept rambling. "I didn't mean for that to sound like I want to keep up a ruse or anything. I was being genuine. We have a spark or some shit. I don't know. I like you. If you like me too, then we should date for real, right? Otherwise, we might regret it. Don't you think?"

He was serious. Marco couldn't quite follow everything he said, but he was serious. "Yes." The word burst out a little louder than Marco liked, but he had to make Valentine's rambling stop. "Yes," he repeated, sounding calmer this time. "I like you and you're right. I'll regret it if I don't pursue that."

A smile exploded across Valentine's face. "Cool." He filled the spot next to Marco on the couch and draped his arm across Marco's shoulders. "Awesome. This is great. I'm excited." They sat there for a second in silence, with Valentine tapping his fingers on his thigh. "What do couples do?"

A loud laugh burst from Marco. He held his side when the laughter wouldn't stop. They were both so goddamn weird. He had no idea what they were doing, and they likely had no business trying at all. Yet Marco couldn't wait to see what happened next. He hadn't felt this alive in years. Being with Valentine was the best time of his life. He wanted more.

Marco's laughter was quickly becoming an addiction for Valentine. He liked the way it made him feel in his chest. Valentine knew he should have called. It wasn't on Marco. He had needed a few days to think. There had to be a reason he had intentionally called notice to

Marco in Vegas, shoving him into the spotlight. Valentine had never shown any real interest in anyone before. It had to be more than just impulse. Valentine clicked with Marco. He had to know it wasn't just him. Now he had no idea where they went from here.

"Let's start small," Marco suggested. "How about I order us dinner and we watch a movie?"

Marco was always offering to pay for things like he wasn't unemployed. It was sweet but unnecessary. "Why don't I order us dinner and you choose the movie?"

"I can afford to buy our dinner."

Valentine shrugged. "I'm sure you can, but I can't choose a movie, so..."

Marco shook his head. He always looked like Valentine made him tired, but then he still let Valentine have his way. "All right. That's a weird thing to say, though. Why can't you choose a movie?"

As he answered, Valentine dug out his phone to open a food delivery app. "I don't watch TV." Valentine clicked around for a full minute before he noticed the silence. He looked up to find Marco staring at him as if he turned purple. "What?"

"Who in the hell doesn't watch TV? Like, ever?"

Valentine shifted uncomfortably. "Sometimes I turn on the news or sports coverage."

"What do you do in your free time?" Marco sounded genuinely dumbfounded.

"I read and work out."

"Reading I get, but working out seems more work-related. I meant solid free time. What do you do to entertain yourself?"

Valentine shrugged. "I go to clubs. Create artisan coffees. Wood burning. Sometimes, I play golf. Sew."

"Wait. You sew?"

The discomfort was really setting in. "I dabble in a lot of things. My mind is too busy to sit still with myself."

Marco's gaze moved over his face. He didn't say anything, and his expression gave nothing away.

"Why are you acting like I'm weird?"

A smile slowly spread Marco's lips. "I don't think you're weird. Well, maybe a little, but you actually make me really glad we met. There are so many layers to you. You fascinate me."

Valentine dropped his gaze to his phone so Marco wouldn't see how moved he was by the confession. He couldn't stop smiling, though. They were still in the stage of getting to know each other. But every time they were together, Marco gave Valentine more reasons to like him. He felt good in Marco's company. Valentine hadn't felt good about anything in a while. For someone who hadn't had a relationship since high school, he was oddly excited to be in one again, because it was Marco. It was like dating a friend. Now all he had to do was make Marco happy too. The poor guy. What had Marco been thinking by telling him yes? Hopefully, he wouldn't regret it. Valentine couldn't promise he wouldn't.

"My dad wants an autograph, by the way."

A laugh burst from Valentine. He just really liked Marco. They would be happy.

Chapter Five

MOM: *WHO IS THIS guy who has you smiling in all the tabloids?*

Valentine: *His name is Marco.*

Mom: *I gathered that from the papers. That's not what I asked.*

Valentine: *He's a thirty-four-year-old ex-Navy pilot. We've been dating for about a month. You'd like him.*

Mom: *A month?!! That's a fucking record for you. When can we meet him?*

BEAUTIFULLY VALENTINED

Valentine: *lol*

Mom: *I'm serious.*

Valentine: *I know. That's why I laughed.*

Mom: **sigh**

Valentine: *So... Want to go to Washington and meet my moms? They won't stop asking.*

Marco: *Only if you want to go to Mississippi to meet my ridiculously over-the-top family.*

Valentine: *I'd be up for that. You can fly us both places.*

Marco: *Damn. What's happening here?*

Valentine: *Don't know. Crazy, right?*

Marco: *We must be.*

Tricia: *I've been talking to all the kids about Christmas. We always have to choose a random day in December because everyone's schedules are crazy. Do you think you could join us on the 21st? I didn't ask Marco because I knew he would drag his feet answering.*

Valentine: *We'll be there. I'll let him fly and he'll agree to anything.*

Tricia: *That boy. I swear, the sky is all he cares about.*

Valentine: *Then I'm happy to give it to him.*

Never in all his years on this planet had Valentine wanted to be with the same person for four months, yet here he was. Seriously, though, Marco was his best friend. He couldn't picture doing anything without him any longer. That was why it fucking irritated him beyond measure that Marco kept going on job interviews like Valentine wouldn't take care of him. Like Valentine *didn't* take care of him. Every time one of Valentine's friends needed a substitute pilot, Valentine got Marco the job. Marco definitely made enough money from those gigs to stop trying to find a job he would hate. Marco wasn't built to sit behind a desk all day with his soul rotting away. It made Valentine want to punch someone just thinking about it. Since he couldn't take a hit himself, he opted to abuse a bag instead.

Valentine's muscles screamed as each hit landed harder. He tried not to relive his days in the ring. Despair waited at the end of that road. Like Marco, Valentine also wasn't made to be just some guy. But damned if he hadn't felt irrelevant as hell since retiring. The guys at the gym kept getting younger. Cockier. Valentine felt like some old workhorse put out to pasture. Today, everything seemed to be under his skin. Marco was at another goddamn interview. Byron still kept blowing up his phone. There was a dude in the ring nearby who kept leaving open his left side, then acting surprised when he got hit. Fuck. It was enough to make him take up heavy drinking.

"Goddamn it. I can't take it anymore." Valentine slapped his gloves on the mat, getting the two fighters' attention before climbing into the ring. "What in the fuck are you doing? Who is training you? You hit like a goddamn truck, then drop your hands, leaving yourself wide open."

The blond looked dumbfounded by the sudden criticism. He spit out his mouthpiece. "No one's training me. I'm just blowing off steam."

Valentine shook his head. "If you're going to do this, do it right. Do you want your brains knocked around in your head? Even if this is just a hobby, you could get hurt if you don't protect your goddamn face. Look." Valentine moved to his side and motioned for him to match Valentine's pose. "Put your guard back in."

The kid did as told and Valentine fixed his stance and showed him where to focus on his elbow placement before the pair went back to sparring. Valentine stayed in the ring but out of the way. A genuine smile pulled at his lips as the guy followed his instructions and finally blocked some hits.

"There you go. Protect yourself. It's not enough to hit hard. You also need to be good at something other than taking a hit. You want to not get hit in the first place."

"You're smiling."

Valentine glanced over at the words. He found Marco waiting outside the ring. His smile grew. "Every time I see you, I smile. Why are you surprised?" Valentine climbed from the ring and stole a quick kiss. "How did your interview go?"

"It pays twelve an hour."

Valentine winced. "Jesus. No one can afford to work for that. I wish you'd stop this." The words were out there before he could call them back.

The line that immediately appeared between Marco's eyebrows let him know he should have kept the words to himself. "What's that supposed to mean?"

If there was one thing Valentine had always been good at, it was doubling down. He led Marco out of earshot of anyone listening. "You don't need to work. I can always find you flying gigs whenever you need the money. Or hell, you have me. There's no reason to keep going to all these pointless interviews."

The way Marco's chest expanded on a deep breath let him know things could go either way at this point. "Your money isn't my money." His tone gave nothing away. "It would kill me if you ever thought I only cared about what you could do for me. Let me have my pride. I have nothing else."

Now Valentine was irritated again. "What do you mean, you have nothing else? You have me."

"We've been together four months."

He didn't like Marco's tone. "So you're dumping me? Is that it? Otherwise, I don't see your point."

Marco pinched the spot between his eyes.

"Do you mind if I get a few more pointers from you?" The blond guy from the ring appeared from nowhere, catching Valentine off guard at just the right moment.

Valentine glanced his way. "Sure. It seems I'm done here anyway."

Marco dropped his hand. He looked tired. The dark circles beneath his eyes were back. "I guess you just made my point. It was only a matter of time before one word from some dude half my age had you running his way."

Before Valentine had time to process the blow, Marco walked away. He limped more than usual today, and Valentine had no clue what just happened. He turned away because he hated that it might have been his fault, but he didn't even know at this point.

The blond didn't seem to notice anything amiss. "I'm Draven, by the way."

Valentine nodded. "Nice to meet you, Draven." It seemed he had all the time in the world to offer the kid a few tips. He might have just ruined everything else in his life.

Marco immediately regretted every angry word. It wasn't Valentine's fault no one wanted to hire him. He had come to L.A. to be near his brother, and nothing felt good anymore except Valentine. Still, sometimes, it felt like life was leaving him behind. Thanks to Valentine, he hadn't completely lost his chance to fly, but when Valentine got bored with Marco, that would be over. Then Marco would still be in this town that he couldn't afford, seeing his twin once in a blue moon. It wasn't like he could spend his free time at The Aviator when everyone there had been with his man at some point. Ugh. He was angry with all the wrong things today. Marco got that. Life was unfair and it always would be. He needed to suck it up and apologize to Valentine. Marco was almost to his car and despair filled him to the point he wanted to break shit. Twelve goddamn dollars an hour. In L.A. What the fuck? It was insulting. He spun and walked right into a hard, wide chest.

Valentine's arms encircled him, holding him together. He kissed Marco's temple. "Tell me how I can fix it."

"I'm sorry." Marco fought the urge to break down and babble like an idiot. His eyes stung. "You're the only good thing in my life, and I didn't mean to take my problems out on you. You didn't deserve that."

"Shhh." Valentine's lips moved to the corner of Marco's mouth. "It's okay. I get it," he said between light kisses. "Everyone wants workers. No one wants to pay. You can't do what you love full time. But here's the thing, you actually can do a different thing you love full time, and I wish you'd hear me out about that."

Despite everything, Marco smiled. Valentine was just so much more than everyone else. He was larger than life and irresistible. Marco's bad mood couldn't compete with Valentine's ego. "What's this other thing I love?"

"Me," Valentine said, sounding every bit as arrogant as Marco expected.

Marco bit his bottom lip to keep from laughing.

Valentine made a dismissive gesture. "Don't look at me like that. I know you haven't said the words, but—lucky for you—you're dating a smart man. You love me and I want nothing more than for you to do me full time."

A snort burst from Marco. He shook his head. "You're insane." Even Marco heard the laughter in voice.

In an instant, Valentine turned completely serious. "Maybe, but I love you. Please stop trying to force yourself into a position you'll hate. I don't know why you're trying to punish yourself, but I have a pretty good idea. Your brother isn't ignoring you. He loves you. It's just that he's married now and has a business to run. Which is cool with you because you have me, and I plan to always be very demanding of your time and attention."

Marco could barely breathe. "You love me?"

"Duh."

Marco still felt overwhelmed and confused. "I don't even know what you're saying to me right now."

Valentine's gaze never wavered from holding Marco's stare. "Move in with me. Let's stop playing like this is some temporary experiment. I'm in love with you. I want you with me."

"I'm in love with you too."

"I know."

A smile snapped to Marco's lips at the cockiness in Valentine's voice. "Okay. Let's do it." He'd be a goddamn fool to say no.

"Woot." Valentine cheered even as their lips met, making Marco laugh... the way he always did. The laughter died away as Marco's back hit his driver's side door of his car. Valentine crowded his space as their tongues played. As always, Marco felt tiny in Valentine's arms. He made the world and all of Marco's problems disappear.

"We're going to your parents' place on the twenty-first for Christmas," Valentine said as he changed directions.

Happiness seized every molecule in Marco's body and held on. He wanted to drag Valentine into his car and show him how much brighter life was because they were together. The thing was, though, he saw Valentine every bit as clearly as Valentine saw him. Retirement was killing him. He needed an outlet.

Marco gently pushed Valentine away and kissed the tip of his nose. "You should head back inside and offer to train that kid. It was nice to see you happy again."

"I have you. I'm always happy."

Marco held Valentine's stare.

Valentine's smile grew. "And you were surprised I love you. No one else sees me at all."

Marco snorted. "Oh, sexy. Everyone sees you. You're too beautiful to miss, but I know you. You love boxing. Try to hang on to what you can. Maybe you can't fight again. That doesn't mean you're done. It doesn't mean you have nothing left to offer the sport. While you're at it, answer Byron's calls. Someone gave him my number, and he's bugging me too now."

Valentine's eyes fell closed, and he touched his forehead to Marco's. They stayed there, breathing in each other's air for much longer than necessary. "I'll go," Valentine said, sounding resigned. "But only if you go to *our* house and start planning your move. I need to know you're waiting for me."

Marco's face hurt from smiling. "I can do that."

Valentine nodded, squishing their foreheads together. "You know the code to get in. Love you."

"Love you too."

Before the final word died on his lips, Valentine was back for more kisses. The

truth hit Marco as Valentine's hold tight-
ened. They had been meant to meet.
Not only that, but they were also heal-
ing each other. Apart, they were just two
men at a crossroads, losing everything
that mattered. Yet they had met exactly
when they needed each other. That was
too much to be a coincidence. He didn't
really believe in a higher power, but at
that moment, he kind of did. Valentine
made him believe in everything, especially miracles.

Chapter Six

THEY HAD BEEN TO Marco's parents' house once together for a brief visit. This was the first time Valentine had met the entire brood at one time. They were loud and rowdy. His sister, Anna, had three kids. Two of which were twins. They were all on the small side and were the center of attention. Valentine had met almost everyone else before at some point. Marco's younger brother, Tito, was the personal bodyguard to a musical legend. So they sometimes found themselves in the same circles.

Tito's husband, Cooper, wasn't someone Valentine had met, but he was shy
and quiet. The way people sheltered
him from everything said a lot. Valentine kept his distance. In fact, Valentine
did his best to stay out of the way in
every scenario. He was a loud person,
but they were louder. Even though he
fit in, he decided his first Christmas with
the family probably wouldn't be the best
time to overwhelm everyone with his
awesomeness. They would learn soon
enough.

With presents opened and food con-
sumed, a majority of the family decided
to go out for a family bike ride. With
Marco's bad leg and Valentine not being
a motorcycle guy, they stayed behind.
Marco gathered snacks so they could
hide in their assigned bedroom for the
rest of the night. Valentine hauled their
luggage from the rental car since they

had been dragged into the house the moment they arrived and hadn't been given a chance to do a thing since. He was ready to change into something comfortable.

Halfway to the back door, Enzo ambushed him. "So now you're coming to family events?"

"You didn't go out with the rest of the family?"

Enzo shook his head at Valentine, pointing out the obvious. "Aric has a headache."

It took everything Valentine possessed to keep from saying he didn't doubt it. This family was a bit much. They were awesome, but exhausting. They held each other's stare. Enzo didn't look happy with him.

"Do you plan to get to the point?"

Enzo shrugged. "You tell me, man. I thought we already talked about this at The Back Porch a while back. Now you're here. Are you really planning to toy with my brother forever?"

Valentine twirled his suitcase, ready to get back to Marco. He didn't truly understand the issue. "I have to say, this is weird. First off, that day at The Back Porch, you said you didn't care what Marco and I did. Plus, you were angry with Marco for not accepting Aric, and now you're pulling the same shit with me. You two have a strange relationship."

"The shit with Aric and my beef with you are not the same," Enzo said without missing a beat. "Marco didn't want to accept Aric because he had unfounded assumptions. I'm not assuming anything. I know you. You've been coming to my club since the day it opened. I know you."

"Uh-huh." Valentine spun the suitcase again. "Do you, though? Please, tell me about myself."

Enzo snorted. "Okay. You're arrogant, quick to boredom, and you'll jump on the first new piece that comes your way. My family is falling in love with you, and you'll be gone before next season's clothing line drops."

Valentine started smiling at "arrogant" and hadn't stopped. "So your family loves me, huh?"

Enzo rolled his eyes.

Valentine didn't give him time to answer. "Your brother has been living with me for over a month." Enzo's expression snapped closed, but it wasn't satisfying enough for Valentine. He kept going. "Yep. He's completely moved in and has stopped job hunting. We both know he'll never be happy behind a desk, and I've got him. I've had all the new pieces and you know what? They all bored me to tears. Marco is my best friend. I love him and he loves me. Since we'll be brothers soon, I'll walk away now and forget this happened. Your brother moved to L.A. for you and you alone, so I hope you two can find a way to be friends again. It matters a lot to him. He needs to know he's forgiven. Either way, I'll be at his side. I hope you will be too."

Valentine tried to steer past Enzo. Enzo stuck his foot out, stopping the suitcase. "What do you mean we'll be brothers? Have you asked Marco to marry you?"

Valentine winked, lifted the suitcase, and walked around Enzo, leaving him behind. Enzo wasn't wrong for the way he felt. He didn't know Valentine. All

Enzo knew was what he had seen and heard at The Aviator. That wasn't Valentine. That wasn't *knowing* him. Valentine had never started anything he didn't finish. He had met Marco, chosen him, and now they would be together for the rest of their lives. He didn't share, and he held himself to the same standard. Enzo would get onboard eventually. Of that, Valentine had no doubts.

Marco wasn't in the kitchen where Valentine had left him, so Valentine headed upstairs. The house was a fairly new build, so Valentine imagined Marco's parents bought the place specifically to have enough room for all their kids to visit and have privacy when they did. The first floor was mostly living and entertainment space: kitchen, living room, den, master bedroom, two bathrooms, and a smaller bedroom for Anna's kids. All the rest of the bedrooms were on the second floor. Each of the five upstairs bedrooms had a full bathroom. Marco's dad had been career military, designing fighter jets for his country. He had made a good life for them. Before learning all of that during their first visit, Valentine had hoped for a hotel room where he could have Marco alone at night. Now he knew a hotel was unnecessary. No one expected them to behave.

Valentine dragged their bags into the bedroom. He caught Marco undressing. Marco was already down to his underwear. "Oh, good. We're skipping the food and getting straight to fucking. My favorite snack of all."

Marco snorted. "I thought you'd be here quicker with our pajama pants. It's time to be lazy."

"Your brother stopped me in the driveway."

Marco grabbed his suitcase and started digging. "Which one?"

Valentine peeled off his shirt and unzipped his bag. "Enzo. He's a little pissed that I'm meeting the fam when it's obvious I'll jump on the first new piece that comes along."

Marco groaned. His sexy green eyes focused on Valentine. "Did he actually say that?"

"Yes, but it doesn't matter." Valentine flashed him a huge smile. "I told him not to worry because we'll be married soon and then he'll see."

Marco blinked. "What?"

Valentine dropped to his haunches and dug around inside his overnight bag. When his fingers wrapped around a velvet box inside, he shifted to one knee. Valentine opened the box.

Marco stared down at the ring, expressionless. "Is this a joke? Is my family going to jump out of the closet and yell 'gotcha' any second?"

"Fuck. I should've set that up just so I could see your face, but no. This is real, gorgeous. I love you. You know I'm not one to play when I want something. I want you. Forever. Not just for as long as you can tolerate me, because—let's face it—I'm not that tolerable. I need to know you'll need a good fucking lawyer to get rid of me. I mean, the best. Like, you may as well keep me, because it's not even worth the trouble."

The way Marco's eyes danced with laughter had Valentine's throat swelling.

"I'm serious," he repeated, sounding hoarse this time. "The only people in this world that really love me are my moms and you. I can't lose that. I can't lose you."

"We've only been together five months."

Valentine didn't give up. "I thought you liked things that go fast."

"How long have you had this ring?"

Valentine shut the box and shifted back to his feet. He knew no when he heard it. Valentine set the box on the dresser and went back to stripping. He found a pair of pajama shorts that he loved. His gaze stayed locked on his task. Valentine was disappointed, but he would try again another day. For now, though, his chest hurt. He couldn't look at Marco, but he saw Marco move from the corner of his eye. Valentine chanced a glance. Marco opened the box and looked inside.

"It's okay," Valentine said in his discomfort. "It's me. I get it. You've been in my life for five months now. I'm sure you've seen there's no one beating down my door to be around me. I'm just... I don't know. Too much or something." While he rambled, Marco slipped the ring on his ring finger.

"It fits."

Valentine didn't respond. He was out of words and his throat burned. Until Marco didn't say yes, Valentine hadn't realized just how badly he wanted to get married.

Marco stroked the ring. "I don't know why I'm surprised. You always know everything about me without me having to say a word."

"Of course I do. You're my best friend."

Marco met Valentine's stare. There were tears in his eyes. "You took me by surprise."

That was fair. "I know we haven't talked about marriage."

Marco shook his head. "I mean you. You took me by surprise. I never expected you. Not the night we met or the first time you texted. I never thought you'd show up at my door with flowers or ask me to move in with you. Every moment with you has been one shock after the other. I never see anything you do coming, and I couldn't be more in love with this life we have together. Of course I'll marry you. You're damn right I want this craziness for the rest of my life. There isn't another soul out there for me but you."

Valentine made the space between them disappear in an instant. He felt too much to speak. Valentine had to act. He couldn't explain the overwhelming emotions consuming him, but he could show Marco how much he meant. Their mouths clashed and all Valentine could think about was how much Marco had saved him. He had been drowning when they met. Silently slipping under. No one had seen or cared. As long as Valentine kept supporting everyone in his life financially in some manner, they didn't care what it cost him. Marco—without knowing him at all—had seen him and saved him. He had loved Valentine and asked for nothing in return. In fact, Valentine knew if he tried fighting again, Marco would kill him because he loved Valentine. Him. Not the money or the fame. He was here right now for Valentine.

"I love you."

Valentine's eyes burned as Marco pulled away just enough to make that confession, as if he'd been having all the same thoughts as Valentine. "I'm so fucking in love with you too."

"Give me your pants. I want your pants."

A chuckle rose in Valentine's throat. "Why? They're too big for you."

Marco snagged the waistband of Valentine's jeans and went to work unbuttoning and unzipping them before pushing them down Valentine's hips. That was always the easy part with his jeans. There was no good size for him. He had thick thighs but a small waist. Marco had to work to peel them down Valentine's thighs. He managed to get that far and then he froze. A sharp gasp cut through the air. Marco hovered between kneeling and standing. They had been together long enough for Valentine to know exactly what happened. There were certain ways Marco couldn't move without his leg seizing.

Valentine kicked his way out of his clothes and snatched Marco from his feet. He quickly carried him to the bed. Marco's eyes flashed with pain. The muscle in his jaw twitched. No doubt he held back screams. Valentine straddled his shins and went to work on his thigh and hip, massaging the muscle while re-aligning the leg.

Marco groaned.

"That's it, baby. I've got you. You know I can make you feel good." Valentine watched Marco's semi hard cock twitch inside his underwear. He hid a smile. Valentine knew his praise sounded sexual. He meant it to be. Valentine needed to distract Marco from the pain. He kept one hand on Marco's thigh, massaging. With the other, he snagged Marco's underwear and dragged it down.

Marco's eyes still flashed with pain, but there was hunger too. "What do you have planned?"

An evil-sounding chuckle fell from Valentine's lips. "I told you. I plan to make you feel good."

"This leg isn't moving again tonight."

Marco's wicked smile grew. "It had better not. I'd hate to have to spank you."

Valentine left Marco's underwear wrapped around his knees. He crawled up Marco's body, holding Marco's stare. "I stare at you a lot more than anyone should. You're sexy as hell."

Marco's fingertips found Valentine's sides as Valentine moved to hover over him. "Same."

Valentine grabbed his dick and rubbed it against Marco's cock.

Marco stifled a whimper.

Valentine did it again. With his weight braced on one arm, he held Marco's stare while playing with their erections. Marco squirmed beneath him, as if the soft brushing of cock on cock wasn't enough. Valentine leaped from the bed.

"No." The word dragged out in disappointment from Marco. "Where are you going?"

"I told you to be still. You're moving. I have to give you more to keep you still."

Valentine grabbed the lube from their toiletries bag and returned to Marco's side. He stood over the bed and lubed Marco's erection. Marco's eyes screamed with hunger. While they were both versatile, Valentine had never bottomed for Marco. Every time things got heated between them, Valentine had to be inside that tight ass. That was the only reason why. Tonight, Marco needed to let Valentine have him in a different way.

Valentine straddled Marco's hips. "Stay still or I'll stop." It would be hard, but he would. He wouldn't let Marco hurt himself.

Marco licked his lips as Valentine held Marco's cock in place and led it toward his asshole. "Are you sure? You've never shown any interest in this before."

A drop of pre-cum rolled down Valentine's erection. "Oh, I'm interested." Even Valentine heard the lust in his voice. His eyes nearly rolled back in his head as he sat on Marco's dick. He loved the mixture of pleasure and pain. Valentine's brain stopped working as he turned inward. He focused completely on the task of riding Marco's cock. Valentine shifted positions until that delicious dick rubbed his happy spot. Then he took what he wanted. Valentine set a steady pace while stroking his cock. He thrust inside his fist while taking every inch of Marco over and over again.

With his head thrown back and his eyes closed, Valentine let the pressure build. It had been a long time since he lost himself like this. He dropped his gaze and met Marco's stare. Marco's cheeks were flushed, and his lips parted on a pant. He stroked Valentine every place he could reach. Valentine jacked his dick faster.

"You make an addict of me. I never get tired of being with you. It gets worse every day. Pretty soon, I won't be happy unless you live on my dick." Valentine moaned. "Or fuck, maybe I need to live sitting on yours."

"I'll take it. You feel amazing." Marco's expression turned dark. "This ass is mine. If anyone else ever touches you,

I'll cut off their hands and your dick. Do you understand me?"

Damn. That was hot. "One time in my ass and you go caveman."

"I've always been possessive. We've just never been engaged. You're mine."

The growl in Marco's voice nearly made him come. Valentine's breath stuttered. "Fuck. I'm about to blow, sexy. Please tell me you're close." Valentine bounced faster. He needed the pleasure only Marco gave him.

"Then blow. I want to feel that tight ass milking me deeper."

Valentine would give him anything. He pumped as fast as he could while Marco's wet cock sawed in and out of his asshole. The pressure built to almost painful. Then everything went silent for half a breath before his body jerked. He bit his bottom lip to stay silent as he shot cum all over Marco's stomach and chest. Valentine fought for air while he kept riding Marco's dick. Marco's fingers dug into Valentine's skin, leaving indentions while he visibly fought to stay still and let Valentine bring him release.

Marco let go and grabbed the headboard. His knuckles turned white. The muscles in his neck strained. He was the most beautiful thing Valentine had ever seen. A loud gasp cut through the air. Marco's body jerked. Satisfaction roared through Valentine. He had done that. Valentine had made this gorgeous man orgasm. It was powerful. Marco's wild gaze met his stare and didn't budge. It was love staring at him. Powerful and real. They were forever. This would be his husband until they grew old and died. He had gotten a miracle.

The way Valentine softened in his sleep always fascinated Marco. More times than he cared to admit, Marco had lain awake for hours, staring. Valentine always looked one of two ways; unapproachably angry or like a kid who had too much candy and caffeine. But when he slept, Valentine became someone new. He looked like an angel. Marco never stopped being blown away by him.

Without thinking, Marco's gaze moved to the ring on his finger. It looked delicate, but Marco didn't doubt for a second Valentine had dropped a small fortune on it. The backs of his eyes stung unexpectedly. He didn't deserve this amazing life that had adopted him when he hadn't been looking. Marco wanted this, though. He would fight and claw to keep it. Every time he thought about Valentine telling him he was his best friend, Marco wanted to weep with joy for the blessings that had come from nowhere. He had never felt less alone.

The floor creaked outside their room and Marco checked the clock. It was eleven p.m., and they hadn't touched the snacks Marco found for them. He bit back a groan and quietly rolled from the bed. If he let food go to waste, his mom wouldn't be happy. He needed to put everything up before it was ruined. Marco found his pajama pants and grabbed Valentine's discarded shirt. It was baggy and comfortable. Plus, it smelled like Valentine, which made him purr inside. Once sufficiently dressed, Marco gathered the food and drinks and sneaked from the room. He didn't run into anyone until he stepped through the swinging door of the walk-in pantry. Enzo was raiding the place.

He started at Marco's appearance. "Shit. Hey. I didn't hear you coming."

Marco chuckled. "Did you think Mom had come to scold you?"

A bright smile lit Enzo's face. "I guess. Funny how you never grow out of certain things. I thought you were asleep."

"Nah." Marco returned an unopened sleeve of butter crackers to their box. "I've just been hanging out in bed, being lazy."

"Can I talk to you?" The question burst from Enzo like he had been holding it back for ages.

Marco didn't need to think about it. "Of course."

"I'm happy for you. I mean, about your whole relationship with Valentine," Enzo clarified. "You both seem really happy, and I don't know why I haven't tried harder to accept him. I like Valentine. Always have. You two deserve this. I don't know why I've been so negative about the entire situation, but he obviously loves you."

Marco shrugged. "You've been worried he'd hurt me."

Enzo held his stare, looking lost. "I really don't understand why we can't go back to the way we used to be."

A smile exploded across Marco's lips. Six months ago, he had felt the same way, but now he knew better. "We grew up. Scary shit, I know." Without thinking, Marco wrapped his arms around Enzo and squeezed. After a moment, Enzo did the same. They hugged for much longer than necessary. Marco had to be honest. "We were toxic as fuck as best friends."

A breathless-sounding laugh burst from Enzo.

Marco didn't stop trying to explain. "We hurt other people and ourselves." Marco stepped back and held Enzo's stare. "I don't know about you, but I'm happier being a better person now. Right before I came downstairs, I was watching Valentine sleep and the truth really sank in like it never has before. I'm what's made me miserable my whole life. While I spent years playing people and searching for the next rush, I was standing in my own way. The reason I'm so happy now is that I just stopped. I let myself be happy without fear and trusted someone besides myself. You'll always be my twin. No one can replace you. I don't want to lose you. That's why

I moved to L.A., but I get Aric will always be more important than me. That's how it's supposed to be."

"Who are you?"

Marco laughed.

A bright smile lit Enzo's face. "I don't think I've said it, but I'm so thankful you moved to L.A., even though we still don't see each other enough. Also, wow. You landed Valentine Hollinger. That's fucking insane."

Marco's laughter doubled. He swiped at his eyes. "I know, right? What the fuck? Is he nuts?"

They both roared with laughter. They couldn't look at each other without laughing harder.

The pantry door swung open. Their mom stood in her housecoat, glaring at them. "For fuck's sake. You two are thirty-five. Don't you two have better halves keeping you in line somewhere? People are trying to sleep."

"Sorry, Mom," they chanted simultaneously, only to burst into another round of loud laughter. Marco felt fuller than he had in years. He still had his brother. They hadn't changed all that much. If anything, they were better now. Happier. He wouldn't want things any other way.

Chapter Seven

Fourteen months later, Valentine's Day...

Shoulder to shoulder, Valentine and Marco stood silently brushing the backs of their fingers against one another, and casting longing looks each other's way. There were too many people around them to say what they were always thinking. They were proud to be together. This day, like every day before it, was better because they were at each other's side through the adventure. There was no one Valentine would rather have with him right now.

"We're coming to you live from Valentine's Rehabilitation and Training Center for their opening day ribbon-cutting. Valentine and Marco Hollinger are here with us to tell us about this new addition to our city. Valentine, what inspired you to start this venture?"

After taking a steadying breath, Valentine pasted on his most charming smile. "Hey, Willow. As with everything good in my life, it started with my husband, Marco." He motioned Marco's way. Marco winked and Valentine's nerves steadied. "One day, I was moping around the house."

"He was being obnoxious, actually."

Valentine chuckled at Marco's interjection. "Yeah, I was bored and being annoying. Marco was like, you have to find something to do with your time. So we sat down and brainstormed. We both feel like we still have a lot to offer. He's ex-military, forced into retirement by an injury. I really didn't want to retire either, but my health wouldn't allow me to continue. So we asked ourselves what we could do to help other people just like us. What better than a training center with veteran—military and athletes—staff and trainers? A place for everyone where they won't be judged and can find a new life. Staying active is key to a longer life, so we're here to help. You can go as slow as you need here, but we're also equipped to train you to compete professionally, if you're interested in that. Whatever you need, we can handle it."

"That sounds amazing." Willow shifted the microphone Marco's way. "Tell us more about what it's like to be married to this guy."

Valentine bit back a laugh at the horror in Marco's expression. He knew Marco had already been terribly nervous about this entire ordeal before the spotlight landed on him. Marco always made him proud, and today was no different. Valentine listened to Marco fight for his life with the well-known shark of a reporter for a minute before coming to his rescue. He checked his watch.

"Sorry to interrupt, Willow. You know how much we appreciate the coverage, but we have a schedule to keep. It's still Valentine's Day, after all. You know, Valentine's," he motioned toward himself, "Day. I have to steal my husband."

The blond blinked at him, looking taken aback. Then a smile exploded across her face. "Of course. It's always interesting talking to you. Good luck on the new venture." She turned back toward the camera and fell into a spiel about the club's offerings and hours. They didn't really need the coverage. Byron had already given him a list ten pages long of athletes interested in being trained by the best. They were already a huge success.

Valentine stole his chance to haul Marco out of there. They would spend some of their free time at their new training center, but they had hired experts to run the place full time. Despite needing an outlet for his overabundance of energy, Valentine was still retired and there was nothing he enjoyed more than his husband.

Marco laughed behind him as Valentine rushed him toward their SUV. "Why are we running away? This is your big day. Don't you want to eat up the spotlight?"

Valentine glanced over his shoulder. "It's *our* big day, but not just because of the training center. It's also our one-year wedding anniversary, in case you forgot."

"I haven't forgotten."

Valentine huffed as he opened the passenger side door for Marco. "Then why haven't you wished me a happy anniversary?"

Marco smiled. It looked unrepentant. "Because we've been busy this morning, and I wanted to wait until things calmed down. You know how handsy you get as soon as the topic turns to us."

Because Marco was right, Valentine crowded his space. "I don't think I can be blamed for being turned on by you." He stole a kiss before slapping Marco's ass. "Now get in the SUV before I embarrass you."

"I'd say that isn't possible, but it's you."

An evil laugh rose in Valentine's throat as he closed the SUV door behind Marco. Damn right. There was no low too low if it made Marco smile.

Valentine quickly made his way to the driver's side and climbed behind the wheel.

Marco's lasted until they pulled from the parking lot. "Where are we headed?"

"To get your present."

Marco groaned. "You spoil me, and it makes me feel guilty. I'm perfectly happy with just like riding your face or something."

A loud laugh burst from Valentine. He never stopped smiling with Marco. "I know you would, but I'm also a thousand percent positive you went all out for our anniversary, so I have to do the same."

Marco didn't respond, letting Valentine know he was right. He had gone big for their first anniversary.

Still, Valentine didn't stop at that explanation. "Plus, we got married on Valentine's Day, so I can't have you feeling cheated. Like I don't want you thinking for the rest of your life that you get fucked on gifts because it's our wedding anniversary."

"Oh, dear. This is about to be ridiculously expensive, isn't it?"

Valentine stared at the road and didn't respond. He didn't want to give anything away. As he pulled into their driveway, Marco's knee bobbed. Valentine glanced his way. "Why are you nervous?"

"It's you. I never know what you'll do."

Valentine put the SUV into park as the garage door slid closed behind them. "What if I promise you it's something small?"

Marco visibly relaxed. "I'd feel a lot better if you did."

"Come on and find out." Valentine jumped from the vehicle without looking back. He couldn't wait to see Marco's face. For over a month, there had been a crew working on his secret project, sneaking around every hour Marco wasn't home. Truthfully, it was something big, but it was their first year. They would never have this one again. Plus, he loved watching Marco flip anytime he spent too much money on him.

Instead of heading for the house, he moved toward a door that led to the backside of the garage into a part of the backyard that couldn't be seen from the house. "I've had a hell of a time keeping this under wraps."

Marco's eyebrows rose. "Okay."

Valentine pulled a piece of paper from his back pocket and grabbed the doorknob with his free hand. "The traditional one-year anniversary gift is paper. So here's a print-off of your registration information with the FAA Aircraft Registry." He threw open the door as he passed the paper Marco's way.

Marco's mouth fell open. He stepped through the door, looking like he might faint or explode. Valentine hadn't figured out which way he would go yet. "You bought me a helicopter."

It wasn't a question, but Valentine treated it as one. "To be fair, I really bought me a helicopter. It's in your name and it is yours, but I never plan to drive again now that you have this bad boy. I'll have you dropping me from the sky all over town, avoiding L.A. traffic. Go check it out."

"You bought me a helicopter," Marco repeated.

Valentine eyed Marco. "Did I break your brain?"

Marco didn't move. His gaze never moved from the small helipad Valentine had built and the fun little helicopter now registered in Marco's name.

"It's really yours. You *can* fly it, right?"

The incredulous look Marco shot him was exactly why Valentine had posed the question. He knew Marco could fly anything.

Valentine smiled. "Seriously, baby. Go look at your new toy. It really is for me too. You know how much I love you taking me up in the air."

Marco rubbed the back of his neck as his gaze moved between Valentine and the helicopter. "It's... this is really amazing. Thank you."

Valentine shooed him toward the aircraft. "Go. Play. I want my gift. The longer you dally, the longer I have to wait. You know patience isn't my strongest virtue."

A smile exploded across Marco's face, and he rushed to check out his gift. Valentine followed and watched as Marco inspected every inch. Pride filled his chest. Money meant nothing compared to Marco. He knew it bothered Marco to have this much money dropped on his gift, but Valentine would get it back in trade. Valentine never let Marco have any peace. He already plotted ways to fuck his sexy husband in the next few minutes. They could probably find a way to christen Marco's new toy.

After a few minutes of checking out everything, Marco looked Valentine's way. His shoulders fell in defeat. "Your gift is nothing like this. You'll be disappointed when you see it."

"Not possible." The words burst from Valentine with all the passion they deserved. The only way Marco could disappoint him would be if he divorced Valentine. Valentine could handle anything else. He bounced, getting impatient. "I do want this gift sometime today, though. You know you married a child. Come on. What did you get me?"

Marco climbed from the helicopter. "I admit I've been stalling. I didn't expect you to rush us home like this. Hopefully, the guy I hired is finished already."

Valentine's curiosity shot through the roof. "What did you do?"

A wicked smile stretched Marco's lips. "Come see." He took Valentine's hand and headed for the house. After they toed off their shoes inside the mud room, Marco set the paper Valentine had given him on the kitchen counter as they cut through. Hand in hand, they headed down the hallway toward their bedroom.

"My gift is in the bedroom? I'm in. Is it a dick in a box? If so, you better not have hired a guy for that. I don't share, and I don't want anyone but you."

Marco snorted and kept going. He forced Valentine to stop moving while he peeked inside the bedroom. "Oh, good. Everything is set." Marco towed Valentine forward. "Tada."

Giddiness rose inside Valentine. He jumped up and down like a kid and happy-clapped. "You got me a sex swing."

"It's custom built to take pressure off my bad leg." He moved to the swing and easily hauled himself upward and into the leather piece in a sexy show of strength. "See? Even if I'm having an off day and everything is locking up, this keeps my leg at the right angle."

Valentine eyed his sexy husband in the perfect position to get fucked. His cock stirred. "Jump out. I want to try something."

Marco unwound himself and climbed out. The moment his feet were on the floor, Valentine snagged the waistband of his pants and easily shoved them down his hips, leaving Marco bare-assed. "Okay. Back in the swing."

Even Valentine heard the desire dripping from each word.

Marco didn't immediately obey. Instead, he pulled Valentine in for a kiss. "Happy anniversary," he whispered as he changed angles and bit Valentine's bottom lip.

Valentine's heart swelled with happiness as their tongues stroked. They hadn't started out traditionally. If anyone asked how they met, they didn't have a cutesy story to tell. Instead, they had an all-encompassing heat that burned like an inferno and a love that eclipsed everything else in their lives. They had a partnership built on understanding, and the ability to see the real version of each other when everyone else remained blind. Marco had been Valentined like no one else ever had before, and Valentine regretted nothing. Never would. He held the other half of his soul, and Valentine was about to fuck him in their brand-new sex swing, AKA the greatest gift ever. This was the third best day of his life. It was time to make another memory in their happily ever after.

Please consider leaving a review at the retailer where you purchased this book. Reviews really help with a book's visibility, which allows me to continue writing more stories. Thank you, Charity.

About the Author

CHARITY PARKERSON IS AN award-winning and multi-published author with several companies. Born with no filter from her brain to her mouth, she decided to take this odd quirk and insert it in her characters.

*Eight-time Readers' Favorite Award Winner
*2015 Passionate Plume Award Finalist
*2013 Reviewers' Choice Award Winner
*2012 ARRA Finalist for Favorite Paranormal Romance

*Five-time winner of The Mistress of the Darkpath

Connect with her online:

*Sign up for her newsletter: https://sendfox.com/charityparkerson
*Join her readers' group on Facebook: http://bit.ly/CharitysTribe
*Website: https://www.charityparkerson.com
*A list of her social media accounts and giveaways all in one place: http://hy.page/charityparkerson

www.ingramcontent.com/pod-product-compliance
Lightning Source LLC
Chambersburg PA
CBHW061244170626
46809CB00007B/2819